The Holiday Handwriting School

Robin Pulver · illustrated by G. Brian Karas

Four Winds Press · New York
Collier Macmillan Canada · Toronto
Maxwell Macmillan International Publishing Group
New York · Oxford · Singapore · Sydney

Four Winds Press, Macmillan Publishing Company

866 Third Avenue, New York, NY 10022

Collier Macmillan Canada, Inc.

1200 Eglinton Avenue East, Suite 200, Don Mills, Ontario M3C 3N1

Printed and bound in Singapore

First American Edition

10 9 8 7 6 5 4 3 2 1

The text of this book is set in 16 point Jensen.
The illustrations are rendered in pencil and watercolor.
Library of Congress Cataloging-in-Publication Data
Pulver, Robin. The Holiday handwriting school/Robin Pulver;
illustrated by G. Brian Karas.   p   cm.
Summary: With Mrs. Holiday's help, the Easter Bunny,
Santa Claus, and the Tooth Fairy learn to improve the
notes they leave children after their visits.
ISBN 0-02-775455-3
[1. Penmanship — Fiction.]   I. Karas, G. Brian, ill.   II. Title.
PZ7.P97325 Ho 1991   [E] — dc20   89-77085 CIP AC

For Barbara —
writer and friend
— R.P.

For my mother and father,
with love
— G.B.K.

Mrs. Holiday met her students
at the schoolhouse door.
"How nice to see you.
    Are you ready for your handwriting class?"

"Yes, we are," Tooth Fairy said.
    The three students
    sat down at their desks.

Easter Bunny said, "Mrs. Holiday,
please treat us the same way
you treat all your students."

"Yes," Santa said,
"whether we are naughty or nice."

"I will try," said Mrs. Holiday.
"Now tell me your problems.
Fairy, would you begin?"

"I … I … scribble!" said Fairy.
Fairy's voice was tinkly,
like a music box.
"Sometimes children leave me notes.
They ask, 'What do you look like?'
'What do you do with the teeth?'
I try to write back.
But it is dark in those bedrooms!
Children move and talk in their sleep!
Then I worry. I hurry. I scribble!

"Also," Fairy whispered,
"I write much, much too small."

"Don't worry," said Mrs. Holiday.
"Many fairies have tiny writing.
But you can learn to write bigger."

Mrs. Holiday turned to Santa.
"What is your problem, Santa?"

Santa pulled on his beard.
"I am too messy!
I like to leave a note for the children
before I dash away.
I want to thank them
for the cookies and milk.
But my gloves get dirty
from sliding down chimneys.
I get soot on the paper.
I eat my snack with one hand
and write with the other.
Then the note is a mess,
with cookie crumbs, milk spots, and soot."

Mrs. Holiday patted Santa's hand. She said,
"The first rule for good handwriting
is to relax!"

Bunny leaped off his seat.
"Relax!
That is not easy for bunnies!
Hippety, hoppety, hippety, hoppety,
all the time, that's me.
I try to write,
'Thank you for the carrots.'
I cannot hold still!
I drop my pencil!
The words jump around the page."
Bunny's ears drooped.
"And I always nibble the eraser off the pencil.
Then I cannot fix my mistakes!"

"Listen, Bunny," said Mrs. Holiday.
"You have paws and not hands.
It is hard to write
with paws.
You should be proud of your writing."
Mrs. Holiday smiled at her students.
"But you can *all* do better."

"Fairy," Mrs. Holiday said.
"I have a present for you."

"Oh! What is it?"
Fairy's wings quivered.

"This ballpoint pen.
  It will help you write fast.
  And look!
  Push this button.
  The pen has a light.
  Now you can write in the dark.
  You will not scribble."

  Fairy hugged the pen.
"It is like a fairy wand!
  Thank you, Mrs. Holiday."
  Fairy began to write.
  The ink was gold—
  just right for a fairy.

"Now, while I help Santa,
   try writing bigger," said Mrs. Holiday.
"This paper has lines to help you, Fairy."

   Mrs. Holiday turned to Santa.
"First," she said,
"take off those gloves."

"But my hands are cold," said Santa,
"from driving reindeer."

"Rub your hands together!" said Mrs. Holiday.
"Then they will be warmer.
 Your writing will be smooth and neat."

Santa took off his gloves.
He rubbed his hands together.
He started to write.
"It works!" said Santa.
"No soot on my paper!
My writing is neater, too."

"And *dear* Santa," said Mrs. Holiday,
"never, never eat cookies
  when you are writing!"

"That will be hard," Santa said.
"But I will eat my cookies
  when I finish."

"Bunny, it is your turn,"
  said Mrs. Holiday.
"You must learn to hold still.
  There is nothing I can give you for that.
  But if you really want to,
  you can hold still."

"I do want to," said Bunny.
"I am going to try and try
   to relax and hold still."

Fairy and Santa stopped writing.
They watched Bunny.

When Bunny started to wiggle,
Santa put a hand on Bunny's back.
"You can hold still," Santa said.
Bunny started to bounce.
Fairy flew to his side.
"You can hold still," she said.
Bunny wrote three lines without hopping.
"I did it!
I did it!"
Bunny hopped all over the room.

"We knew you could," said Mrs. Holiday.
"But one more thing, Bunny.
  Always eat a carrot before you begin.
  Then you will not nibble your eraser."

"Hurray!" said Bunny.

"No more handwriting problems," said Fairy.

"It must be time for cookies!" said Santa.

Mrs. Holiday brought out a tray
of cookies and milk
and carrots
and tiny fairy cheeses.
She said, "I am happy
I could help you.
But I am a little sad,
because I do not know
if I will see you again."

Fairy, Santa, and Bunny
whispered together.

"Mrs. Holiday," Fairy said,
"when you wake up in the morning,
look under your pillow."

After their snack,
they all hugged good-bye.

Mrs. Holiday went home to bed.
In the morning,
she looked under her pillow.
She found a dirty glove,
a nibbled carrot,
and a tiny tooth.
With them was a note:

We love you,
Mrs. Holiday. We
will visit you
next year.
Fairy Santa
Bunny